THE NORTHWEST DIVISION

BY TED BROCK AND JOHN WALTERS

Published in the United States of America by
The Child's World® • PO Box 326
Chanhassen, MN 55317-0326

800-599-READ • www.childsworld.com

ACKNOWLEDGEMENTS

The Child's World®: Mary Berendes,
Publishing Director

Editorial Directions, Inc.: E. Russell Primm, Editorial
Director and Line Editor; Katie Marsico, Managing
Editor; Caroline Wood, Editorial Assistant; Susan
Hindman, Copy Editor; John Barrett, Proofreader;
Tim Griffin, Indexer; Kevin Cunningham, Fact
Checker; James Buckley Jr. and Jim Gigliotti,
Photo Reseachers and Photo Selectors

Manuscript consulting and photo research by
Shoreline Publishing Group LLC.

The Design Lab: Kathleen Petelinsek,
Design and Page Production

Photos:
AP: 23
Andrew D. Bernstein/NBAE/Getty: 7, 34, 41, 45
Bettmann/Corbis: 9
Nathaniel S. Butler/NBAE/Getty: 32
Darron Cummings/AP: 2
Tim DeFrisco/Allsport/Getty: 10
Garrett W. Ellwood/NBAE/Getty: 12, 13
Focus on Sport/Getty: 24
Sam Forencich/NBAE/Getty: 5
George Frey/AFP/Getty: 37
Noah Graham/NBAE/Getty: 26
Andy Hayt/NBAE/Getty: 18, 30
Ken Levine/Allsport/Getty: 15
Melissa Majchrzak/NBAE/Getty: 16
Eric Miller/Reuters/Corbis: Cover
Jim Mone/AP: 20
NBA Photo Library/NBAE/Getty: 22, 29
Rich Pedroncelli/AP: 1
Rich Pilling/NBAE/Getty: 38
Ken Regan/NBAE/Getty: 21
Jeff Reinking/NBAE/Getty: 4
Elaine Thompson/AP: 33
Steve Wilson/AP: 36

**LIBRARY OF CONGRESS
CATALOGING-IN-PUBLICATION DATA**

Brock, Ted.
  The Northwest Division / by Ted Brock
and John Walters.
      p. cm. — (Above the rim)
  Includes index.
  ISBN 1-59296-527-X (library bound : alk. paper)
  1. National Basketball Association—History—Juvenile
literature. 2. Basketball—West (U.S.)—History—
Juvenile literature. I. Walters, John (John Andrew)
II. Title. III. Series.
  GV885.515.N37B74   2006
  796.323'640973—dc22
  2005026205

TABLE OF CONTENTS

INTRODUCTION

I n the larger picture that is the history of the National Basketball Association (NBA), the Northwest Division is one of the
new kids on the block.

Sure, each NBA division had a new look in 2004–05, when the
league increased to 30 teams (with the addition of the Charlotte
Bobcats) and aligned itself in six divisions of five teams for the first
time. But not only was the Northwest Division a new creation that
season (taking three teams from the old Midwest Division and two

**Rashard Lewis and the Sonics celebrated after winning the
first Northwest Division title in 2005.**

The Trail Blazers (in the white uniforms) and Jazz are two historically
successful franchises that have fallen on hard times recently.

teams from the Pacific Division), its teams cumulatively have a
shorter history than most of the other divisions in the league.

Don't let that relative inexperience fool you, though. While
the teams of the Northwest—the Denver Nuggets, Minnesota
Timberwolves, Portland Trail Blazers, Seattle SuperSonics, and Utah
Jazz—may be short in years, they're already getting long on tradition.

The SuperSonics are the division's oldest NBA team, having
joined the league in 1967. Denver also began its history that season
(it was known as the Rockets for the first seven years of the fran-

chise's existence), although it played nine years in the now-defunct American Basketball Association (ABA) before joining the NBA. In 1970, the Trail Blazers joined the league as an **expansion team,** and the Jazz (then located in New Orleans) were another addition four years later. The Timberwolves, an expansion team in 1989, are the youngest team in the division.

Northwest Division teams can boast of past superstars such as the Nuggets' Alex English, Dan Issel, and David Thompson; the Trail Blazers' Clyde Drexler and Bill Walton; the SuperSonics' Lenny Wilkens; and the Jazz's Pete Maravich, Karl Malone, and John Stockton. Plus there have been all-time great coaches such as Wilkens, Larry Brown, Jack Ramsay, and Jerry Sloan. And contemporary stars like the Timberwolves' Kevin Garnett and the Nuggets' Carmelo Anthony are among the biggest names in the NBA.

Seattle captured the **inaugural** Northwest Division title by winning 52 regular-season games in 2004–05 and edging Denver by three games, with Minnesota not far behind. We'll tell you all about the Northwest teams that season—as well as in past seasons—and what the future may hold in the pages ahead.

Team	Year Founded	Home Arena	Year Arena Opened	Team Colors
Denver Nuggets	1967	Pepsi Center	1999	Red, blue, and gold
Minnesota Timberwolves	1989	Target Center	1990	Blue, green, and silver
Portland Trail Blazers	1970	Rose Garden	1995	Scarlet, black, and white
Seattle SuperSonics	1967	Key Arena	1995	Green, burgundy, yellow, and bronze
Utah Jazz	1974	Delta Center	1991	Purple, blue, green, copper, and black

CHAPTER ONE

THE DENVER NUGGETS

The Nuggets' past and present met at All-Star Weekend in 2005. That's Hall of Famer Alex English on the left and current star Carmelo Anthony on the right.

n 1976, the ABA took its red, white, and blue basketball and went home. After nine seasons, the ABA—famous for this tricolored ball, which it used instead of the traditional orange one— disbanded. Four of its franchises—the Denver Nuggets, the Indiana Pacers, the New York Nets, and the San Antonio Spurs—joined the

NBA. The Nuggets were among the best of the ABA refugees.

Denver went 50–32 and won the Midwest Division in 1976–77. That team boasted three stars: center Dan Issel, forward Bobby Jones, and guard David "Skywalker" Thompson, who earned his nickname from his gravity-defying dunks. Thompson was also a prolific scorer. Four times, he finished among the top six in the league in scoring.

The Nuggets, however, became linked to scoring and letdowns. Coach Doug Moe arrived in 1981, and in his first full season, 1981–82, the Nuggets established a new NBA mark for scoring, averaging 126.5 points per game. Unfortunately, they set another record for points allowed, 126.0 per game. They are still the only team to score at least 100 points in all 82 games of a season. They also surrendered at least 100 points in every game, finishing 46–36.

The 1982–83 Nuggets were about the same. Forwards Alex English (28.4 points per game) and Kiki Vandeweghe (26.7) finished one-two in the NBA in scoring, but the Nuggets, who went 45–37 during the regular season, were eliminated in the second round of the **playoffs** by San Antonio. During the 1983–84 season, Denver scored 184 points in three overtimes against the Portland Trail Blazers—and lost, 186–184.

Moe departed in 1990. His replacement, Paul Westhead, promised just as much offense. But again, the Nuggets played

High-flying David Thompson was nicknamed "Skywalker."

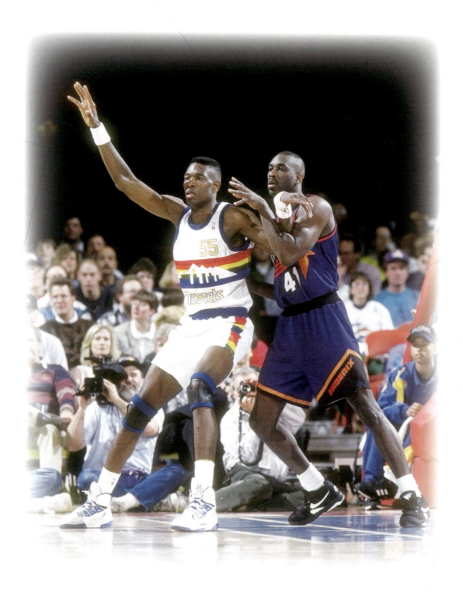

Center Dikembe Mutombo posts up down low.

poor defense. They started out 0–7, surrendering no fewer than 135 points in any of the losses. In one of them, the Phoenix Suns torched Denver for 107 first-half points, an NBA record. Denver again allowed 100 points in all 82 games (no other franchise has ever done that) and set a record for points allowed per game, 130.8. That

1990–91 team finished 20–62, the poorest record in the league.

That began a lengthy dry spell in which Denver finished above the **.500 mark** only one time in a 13-season span. The Nuggets even turned to Issel, their former star center and a member of basketball's Hall of Fame, as coach for two separate stints of two-plus seasons, but he couldn't right the ship.

One highlight of the 1990s, though, was the play of Dikembe Mutombo, a 7-foot-2 center from the Democratic Republic of the Congo. He led the league in blocked shots for three consecutive seasons, was twice named to the All-Star team, and was named the league's Defensive Player of the Year for the 1994–95 season. In 1994, the number-eight seeded Nuggets defeated the number-one seeded Seattle SuperSonics in the playoffs. No eighth-seeded team has beaten a number-one seed, before or since.

Except for a notably disastrous 11–71 season in 1997–98, the Nuggets largely seemed to have been forgotten by the rest of the league. Then, under second-year coach Jeff Bzdelik in 2003–04, Denver made its presence known again. After winning only 17 games the previous season, the Nuggets improved a whopping 26 games and reached the postseason for the first time in nine years.

A number of players had good seasons for Denver that year, including guards Andre Miller and Voshon Leonard, and forward-center Marcus Camby. But the key component in the Nuggets' rise

In 1993, guard Mahmoud Abdul-Rauf made 81 consecutive free throws, the second-longest streak in NBA history. Micheal Williams of the Minnesota Timberwolves had the longest streak—97—but one week after his ended, so did Abdul-Rauf's. Abdul-Rauf's .956 free-throw percentage (219 of 229) in the 1993–94 season is the second-best single-season mark, behind Calvin Murphy's .958.

Veteran coach George Karl (right) took the Nuggets to the 2004–05 playoffs.

Since the NBA began playing 82 regular-season games in 1976, the 2003–04 Nuggets are the only team to make the playoffs the year after failing to win 20 games (they won 17 games in 2002–03).

was rookie forward Carmelo Anthony. The third overall pick in the 2003 NBA draft (behind Cleveland's LeBron James and Detroit's Darko Milicic), Anthony averaged a team-leading 21.0 points per game and was a league All-Rookie first team selection.

With high hopes for 2004–05, the team started slowly, and Bzdelik was let go. He eventually was replaced by veteran NBA coach George Karl, and the Nuggets caught fire. They won 32 of 40 regular-season games to finish in second place in the new Northwest Division with a 49–33 record, and they qualified for the playoffs for the second consecutive year.

The season ended with a loss in the first round of the postseason to eventual NBA champion San Antonio. But with Anthony, who led the club again by averaging 20.8 points per game and had become one of the league's top young players, the Nuggets clearly had struck gold.

Carmelo Anthony has the Nuggets' fortunes looking up.

The history of the Minnesota Timberwolves can easily be divided into two eras: pre-Kevin Garnett and post-Kevin Garnett. Before this gifted player arrived in 1995 straight out of high school, the T-Wolves were a typical expansion ball club. Their limited talent could barely win 25 games in a season. Since Garnett donned a Minnesota jersey, however, the T-Wolves have become an attraction wherever they play, and they regularly visit the postseason.

The Minnesota franchise came into being in 1989. The state's 842 city councils voted for the name Timberwolves over the other choice, Polars. The T-Wolves began play in the Metrodome, home to the Minnesota Twins and Vikings. Minnesota had not had an NBA franchise since the Minneapolis Lakers, who won five NBA titles, moved to Los Angeles following the 1958–59 season.

Guard Micheal Williams converted an NBA-record 97 consecutive free throws from the end of the 1992–93 season through the early part of the 1993–94 season.

The T-Wolves made their NBA debut at home before 35,427 fans. They lost to the Chicago Bulls 96–84, as Michael Jordan drained 45 points. It would take 15 more losses and eight seasons before Minnesota would at last defeat Chicago.

The fans were Minnesota's MVP during the inaugural 22–60 campaign. On April 17, 1990, for the final home game, 49,551 fans swept through the turnstiles. That crowd, the third-largest for a single

Tony Campbell was the expansion Timberwolves' top scorer in 1989–90.

game in NBA history, allowed Minnesota to establish a new single-season attendance record average of 26,160 fans per game. The following season, Minnesota moved into its new and current home, the Target Center.

Those early T-Wolves teams were neither good nor easy to cheer for. Christian Laettner, Minnesota's

The Timberwolves have retired only one jersey number, 2. That number belonged to Malik Sealy, who died in a car crash in 2000.

Kevin Garnett is a perennial All-Star.

top pick in the 1992 draft and the only collegiate member of America's first Olympic "Dream Team," always wore a scowl. He was once suspended for a game for screaming at an assistant coach during a practice.

The following season, Minnesota used its first pick to select Isaiah Rider. He arrived late for his own introductory press conference. Things went downhill from there.

In 1995, Garnett, a senior at Farragut Academy in Chicago, made himself eligible for the NBA draft. Many teams were skeptical; 20 years had passed since a high school player had jumped directly to the NBA. Kevin McHale, the former Boston Celtics' Hall of Fame forward who was then (and still is) the T-Wolves' general manager, took a chance on Garnett. He selected the 18-year-old with the fifth overall pick in the draft.

McHale's gamble has paid off. Garnett, the **prototype** of the modern player, is nearly 7 feet tall, but can dribble like a point guard, shoot like an off-guard, and rebound and defend like a power forward. In his first 10 seasons, he has

On February 2, 1990, Tony Campbell scored 44 points against the Boston Celtics. That stood as a club record (it was tied by Wally Szczerbiak on April 13, 2003) for 15 years until Kevin Garnett scored 47 points against Phoenix on January 4, 2005.

**Young guard Stephon Marbury made an immediate
impact, but eventually was traded.**

been named to the All-Star team eight times. In 2003, he was named
MVP of the All-Star contest in Atlanta.

In 1996, Minnesota drafted guard Ray Allen and then traded
Allen and a draft pick for point guard Stephon Marbury. Coached by
Flip Saunders, Minnesota cleared three hurdles during the 1996–97
season: the T-Wolves beat Chicago for the first time; they had their
first All-Star representatives (forwards Tom Gugliotta and Garnett);
and they advanced to the playoffs with a 40–42 record. Minnesota,

however, was swept by the Houston Rockets in the first round three games to none.

In 1999, the realities of NBA payrolls and ego caused the franchise to take a step backward. Before that season, Garnett had been signed to the largest contract in NBA history, worth approximately $120 million. Jealousy ensued.

Marbury, lightning-quick and a great **assists** creator, was unhappy about playing second fiddle to Garnett. He was traded to the New Jersey Nets midway through the season. (Marbury flourished in New Jersey, finishing among the top 10 in the league in both scoring and assists.) Gugliotta, a **free agent,** signed with the Phoenix Suns before the season began, for far more cash than McHale was willing—or able—to pay him. Minnesota obtained steady Terrell Brandon to replace Marbury. At power forward, Joe Smith, who had been the first player taken in the 1995 draft (four spots ahead of Garnett), replaced Gugliotta. Minnesota stumbled, however, finishing with a .500 record.

The following season the T-Wolves drafted a legitimate second scoring option. Wally Szczerbiak, a 6-foot-7 forward, was named to the All-Rookie first team. He is a career 15-points-per-game scorer and, after Garnett, has become the T-Wolves' most vital player.

The Timberwolves qualified for the postseason eight consecutive seasons under coach Flip Saunders, though they didn't win a postseason series until 2004. That year, Minnesota beat Denver and Sacramento in the playoffs before falling to the Lakers in six games

Longtime NBA assistant Dwane Casey was hired as the Timberwolves' head coach for the 2005–06 season. His only previous head-coaching experience was in Japan in the early 1990s.

Wally Szczerbiak has proved to be an effective complement to Kevin Garnett.

Through 2005, Kevin Garnett had averaged at least 20 points, 10 rebounds, and 5 assists per game for six consecutive seasons. Only Larry Bird ever accomplished the feat in as many as five straight years.

in the conference finals. Garnett was named the NBA's MVP after scoring 24.2 points per game.

After that, expectations were high for 2004–05. But when the Timberwolves stood below the .500 mark after 51 games, Saunders was fired. McHale stepped out of the front office to coach the team and, though Minnesota improved, the Timberwolves finished one game out of a playoff berth. Former Seattle SuperSonics assistant coach Dwane Casey was hired to coach the team beginning in 2005–06.

CHAPTER THREE

THE PORTLAND TRAIL BLAZERS

The Portland Trail Blazers were named in honor of the westward exploration led by Lewis and Clark, whose travels in 1804–06 took them from the mouth of the Missouri River to what is now the northwest tip of Oregon.

The first Trail Blazers teams were coached by Rolland Todd and led by forward Geoff Petrie, who later would become the team's general manager. The team began its quest in 1970–71, its first season, with

The earliest Blazers' teams featured back-to-back NBA Rookies of the Year. In 1970–71, forward Geoff Petrie shared the award with Dave Cowens. The next year, it was forward Sidney Wicks who won.

Jack Ramsey coached Portland to the NBA championship in his first season with the club.

a 29–53 record. Seven years later, the Blazers were NBA champions.

After struggling with four coaches in six seasons, the team hired Dr. Jack Ramsay. His first season in Portland was the third one for center Bill Walton, the NBA's number-one draft pick in 1974 and a two-time National Collegiate Athletic Association (NCAA) champion at University of California, Los Angeles (UCLA). The Blazers, with a supporting cast that

Forward Maurice Lucas was a force on offense for
the Trail Blazers' NBA champions in 1976–77.

**Center Bill Walton (No. 32) and the Trail Blazers beat
Julius Erving and the 76ers in the 1977 NBA Finals.**

included forward Maurice Lucas and guards Dave Twardzik and Lionel Hollins, beat the Julius Erving–led Philadelphia 76ers in the **NBA Finals** in six games.

Ramsay's coaching years in Portland brought more postseason appearances but no return to the title round. In 1983, the team drafted Clyde "the Glide" Drexler, who would become a perennial

"Blazermania" gripped the Pacific Northwest beginning in the 1970s. From the spring of 1977, the Trail Blazers' championship season, through the mid-1990s, every Portland home game was sold out.

All-Star. He played 11 ½ years in Portland and would be a key part of the Blazers' return to the NBA Finals in 1989–90—but not under Ramsay, who was fired in 1986. He was replaced by Mike Schuler, who took the club to a 49–33 record in 1986–87 and was named NBA Coach of the Year.

In 1988, owner Larry Weinberg sold the Blazers to Paul Allen, a co-founder of Microsoft. Rick Adelman took over as head coach in 1988–89, and the Blazers, led by Drexler, power forward Buck Williams, and point guard Terry Porter, reached the NBA Finals the following season before losing to Detroit.

In 1989, the Blazers added power forward Jerome Kersey. The following season (1990-91), they were knocked out of the playoffs in the Western Conference Finals by the Lakers, but they got back in the NBA Finals in 1991–92. After being eliminated from the playoffs in the next two years, the Blazers fired Adelman and hired P. J. Carlesimo to coach a team that now had Rod Strickland at point guard, Harvey Grant at power forward, and small forward Cliff Robinson as its scoring leader.

Clyde "the Glide" Drexler soared above the competition.

**Guard Sebastian Telfair is one of several promising
youngsters on the Trail Blazers' roster.**

The Blazers traded Drexler in 1994–95, the club's last season at
Portland Memorial Coliseum before moving to its jazzy new digs, the
Rose Garden. In 1995–96, Arvydas Sabonis, a 31-year-old Lithuanian
rookie center who had played six years in the Spanish League, joined
the team. Soon, there was another round of roster changes. Out went
Strickland and Grant in a trade with Washington for power forward
Rasheed Wallace. Portland's new shooting guard was Isaiah Rider

and its new point guard was Kenny Anderson. After yet another first-round playoff exit, its new head coach was Mike Dunleavy.

Damon Stoudamire, a Portland native, became the Blazers' point guard in Dunleavy's first year. The following year, 1998–99, Portland made it to the Western Conference Finals. In 1999–2000, the Blazers picked up veteran small forward Scottie Pippen and made it to the Western Conference Finals before losing to the Lakers in Game 7.

Things came unglued in 2000–01, as the Blazers went 8–14 at the end of the regular season and were eliminated by the Lakers in the first round of the playoffs. With Maurice Cheeks coaching the next two years, the Blazers made the playoffs both times, after similar dull efforts in the latter part of the regular seasons. Still, Portland's trip to the playoffs in 2002–03 would be the team's 26th playoff appearance in 27 years.

Unfortunately, it would also be the last for a while. The Blazers fell to .500 in 2003–04 and missed the postseason, then plummeted to 27–55 in 2004–05 for their worst record since the earliest days of the franchise.

The popular Cheeks was fired late that season, and the club went into full rebuilding mode, letting veterans such as Stoudamire and Shareef Abdur-Rahim leave via free agency. Former Seattle coach Nate McMillan was hired to lead a club whose future hinged more on the play of youngsters such as guard Sebastian Telfair, forward Zach Randolph, and teen **swingman** Martell Webster.

The Trail Blazers selected high school stars with their top pick in three consecutive drafts: Travis Outlaw (2003), Sebastian Telfair (2004), and Martell Webster (2005).

THE SEATTLE SUPERSONICS

Seattle's NBA franchise got its name from the town's leading industry, jet aircraft manufacturing. When the SuperSonics began play in 1967–68, the nickname fit perfectly with the expanded travel among pro basketball cities.

The Sonics struggled in their early years and got their first **bona fide** superstar when forward Spencer Haywood joined the club toward the end of the 1970–71 season. It took the brilliance of Lenny Wilkens—who eventually became the NBA's all-time winningest coach—to bring the league championship to Seattle. Wilkens was a player-coach for the team for three seasons beginning in 1969–70. He left in a trade and then returned as coach in 1977–78, after the team had tried coaches Tom Nissalke, Bucky Buckwalter, Bill Russell, and Bob Hopkins.

"Downtown" Fred Brown set a club record when he scored 58 points against the Warriors on March 23, 1974. Brown, one of the most popular players in club history, was the captain of the Sonics' 1979 champions.

By then, the Sonics had gathered their first high-quality team, which included long-range scoring threat Fred "Downtown" Brown, guard Slick Watts, and rookie center Jack Sikma. Under Wilkens, the Sonics made it to the NBA Finals, where they forced the Washington Bullets to Game 7 before losing.

In 1978–79, the Sonics won the NBA title after posting their first 50-plus game-winning season (52–30) and their first Pacific Division title. In the finals,

Guard Dennis Johnson was a key member of the Sonics' NBA champs in 1979.

they lost the first game to Washington and then won the next four games. Defense was the team's calling card, and its starting lineup included Dennis Johnson and Gus Williams in the backcourt, Sikma at center, and forwards Lonnie Shelton and John Johnson.

Owner Sam Schulman sold the team to Barry Ackersley in 1983. By 1984–85, Wilkens' last year as head coach before moving to the front office, his

The Sonics were just 5–17 in 1977–78 when Lenny Wilkens took over as head coach. They went 42–18 the rest of the way and advanced to the NBA Finals.

Gary Payton became a fixture at point guard for the Sonics.

teams had gone 478–402.

The 1983–84 season brought forward Tom Chambers, a free agent from San Diego. New coach Bernie Bickerstaff's first season ended with a 31–51 record. A year later, Sikma was traded, and the team rode the talents of Chambers, forward Xavier McDaniel, three-point shooter Dale Ellis, and point guard Nate McMillan back to the playoffs.

Rebounding wizard Michael Cage came in 1988–89, and the next season, Bickerstaff's fifth and last, brought high-school standout Shawn Kemp to the Sonics' frontcourt. Former Boston point guard K. C. Jones, who had coached the Celtics to two titles in the 1980s, became Seattle's head coach in 1990–91. That year, the team also welcomed point guard Gary Payton, a first-round draft pick who would become the team's central figure for 12 seasons.

Jones' one year as coach resulted in a one-round trip to the playoffs and set the table for the team's rebirth under new head coach George Karl in 1991–92. Karl's pressing, trapping, double-teaming outfit added veteran forward Sam Perkins, forward Detlef Schrempf, and guard

While in Seattle from 1973 to 1978, bald-headed guard "Slick" Watts popularized the use of the headband among NBA players.

Seattle fought Michael Jordan and the mighty Bulls toe-to-toe in the 1996 NBA Finals.

> **The high-scoring Sonics of 1986–87 became the first NBA team ever to boast of three players who averaged 23 or more points per game (Dale Ellis, Tom Chambers, and Xavier McDaniel). Seattle surprised the league that year by advancing to the conference finals.**

Hersey Hawkins over the next three years. In 1995–96, the Sonics won 64 regular-season games en route to the NBA Finals, where they lost to Michael Jordan and the Chicago Bulls in six games.

In 1996–97, the Sonics became the third NBA team ever to win 55 games or more in six consecutive seasons. Then in 1998, Karl was replaced as head coach by Paul Westphal, and the Sonics missed the playoffs for the first time in nine years.

The 1998–99 season signaled the arrival of small forward Rashard Lewis, and the team returned

Luke Ridnour (No. 8) and Rashard Lewis (No. 7) give Sonics' fans lots to cheer about.

to the playoffs in 1999–2000. In 2000–01, former point guard McMillan replaced Westphal as head coach.

In March 2001, the Ackersley Group sold the ever-changing Sonics franchise to the Basketball Group of Seattle LLC. The last trace of the Karl era left town in 2002–03, when the team traded the brash, self-promoting Payton to Milwaukee for superstar shooting guard Ray Allen. Brent Barry moved to point guard, and the Sonics began shaping their return to past glory.

That transformation took a huge step forward in 2004–05. After hovering near the .500 mark in most of McMillan's first four seasons at the helm, Seattle improved to 52–30 and won the Northwest title

Ray Allen had another All-Star season in 2004–05.

Seattle opened the
2003–04 regular
season by playing
two regular-season
games against the
Los Angeles Clippers
in Japan. The Sonics
won both games.

in the division's first year of existence. The sharp-shooting Allen, who averaged a team-leading 23.9 points per game, and Lewis earned All-Star selections that year. Second-year point guard Luke Ridnour also showed signs of developing into an NBA star by averaging 10.0 points and a team-leading 5.9 assists per game. After the season, McMillan left to coach division-rival Portland, and former assistant Bob Weiss, a player for the original Sonics in the 1960s, became head coach.

CHAPTER FIVE

THE UTAH JAZZ

I f you were to create an all-time All-NBA team strictly by the five positions (point guard, shooting guard, small forward, power forward, and center), you could make a strong argument that two of the five players would be Karl Malone and John Stockton of the Utah Jazz.

Stockton, a point guard, was drafted by the Jazz in 1984. Malone, a power forward, was selected by the Jazz in 1985. Through the 2002–03 season, the pair were teammates. Then Stockton retired, and Malone signed with the Los Angeles Lakers as a free agent. But no two players have remained together on the same team for a longer period (18 seasons) in league history.

Individually, Stockton and Malone have rewritten the NBA record book. The 6-foot-1, clean-cut Stockton is the league's all-time leader in assists (15,806) and steals (3,625). Stockton led the NBA in assists for nine straight seasons, a league record, from 1988 to 1996. Most experts consider either Stockton or Earvin "Magic" Johnson to be the greatest point guard ever.

The 6-foot-9 Malone is number one all-time in free throws made (9,787) and attempted (13,188), is sixth in total rebounds (14,968), and 10th in scoring average (25.0 points per game). "The Mailman,"

On November 27, 1996, the Jazz posted the greatest comeback in NBA history. Utah trailed the Denver Nuggets by 36 points but rallied to win, 107–103.

The Jazz hold the team record for most consecutive free throws made in a game: 39. Utah set the record playing the Portland Trail Blazers on December 7, 1982.

as he was known, was number two in total points (36,928 points), trailing only Kareem Abdul-Jabbar. Malone, who won the league MVP award in 1997 and 1999, was simply the best power forward ever to lace up a pair of sneakers.

Stockton and Malone led the Jazz to five Midwest Division titles (they tied for a sixth in 1989–90 with San Antonio) and two trips to the

Karl Malone was known as "The Mailman" because he always delivered.

Point guard John Stockton passed his way into the NBA record book.

NBA Finals. Those journeys, in 1997 and 1998, were spoiled by the incomparable Michael Jordan and the Chicago Bulls. But no team ever put more of a scare into the Bulls than the Jazz.

The Jazz came into the league as an expansion franchise, the New Orleans Jazz, in 1974. The marquee player was "Pistol" Pete Maravich, a superior passer and shooter. Pistol Pete led the league in scoring in 1976–77 by averaging 31.1 points per

Mark Eaton was a limited offensive player who did not even start while at UCLA. Still, he led the NBA in blocked shots in four different seasons and was named Defensive Player of the Year twice.

Of his numerous honors, Karl Malone was twice an All-Star Game MVP (once co-MVP with John Stockton) and was named to the All-NBA first team more times (11) than anyone else in league history.

game. On one evening that season, Maravich scored 68 points against the New York Knicks.

In 1979, the Jazz moved to Salt Lake City and the Midwest Division. The key players there included forward Darrell Griffith, alias "Dr. Dunkenstein." He was the 1981 Rookie of the Year. Though only 6-foot-5, forward Adrian Dantley powered to the hoop enough times to twice lead the league in scoring, in 1980–81 and 1983–84.

The 1983–84 season was one of many firsts for the Jazz. Led by colorful coach Frank Layden, Utah won the Midwest Division (45–37) for the first time. Layden wore outlandish clothes, weighed somewhere above 300 pounds, and always had fun. Once, as the Jazz were being creamed by the Los Angeles Lakers, Layden left the arena. As his team was playing

Guard Pete Maravich was inducted into basketball's Hall of Fame in 1987.

John Stockton missed just 22 games in 19 seasons. Karl Malone's attendance rate was even better. "The Mailman" missed only 10 games in 18 seasons with Utah.

out the final minutes, Layden could be seen eating a sandwich at the hotel coffee shop.

During that 1983–84 season, the Jazz also became the first and only team to have four different players lead the league in a major statistical category. Besides Dantley, Griffith had the highest percentage in the NBA in three-point field-goals (.361). Guard Rickey Green led the league in steals (2.65 per game). Big 7-foot-4 center Mark Eaton led the league in blocked shots (4.28 per game).

Jerry Sloan, who once played for Chicago, succeeded Layden as coach in 1988, and he has been as permanent a resident with the Jazz as Stockton and Malone once were.

In the early 1990s, Utah was a terrific team that was never able to clear the hurdle of a Western Conference title. Finally in 1997, the Jazz did just that. Stockton's buzzer-beating three-pointer in Game 6 of the conference finals against the Houston Rockets sent the Jazz into the NBA Finals.

In both 1997 and 1998, the Jazz met the Bulls for the NBA championship. Both years, Utah pushed Chicago to six games. Also in both years, a heroic effort by Michael Jordan made the difference.

While never winning a ring, Stockton, Malone, and Sloan (who entered his 18th season as coach in 2005–06) set an unofficial NBA record for sustained excellence. From 1988–89, their first season together, through 2002–03, the Jazz did not suffer a losing season.

Since the departure of its two superstars, Utah has struggled. In the first year after the Stockton-Malone era, the Jazz managed to win 42

Forward Carlos Boozer was the Jazz's top scorer (17.8 points per game) in the 2004–05 season.

games, although they missed the playoffs. In 2004–05, however—the first season of the Northwest Division—Utah went just 26–56 and finished in last place.

The new stars are forwards Carlos Boozer, who averaged a team-leading 17.8 points and 9.0 rebounds in 2004–05, and Andrei Kirilenko, although both missed considerable time to injury that season. The Jazz hope they can lead the team to old heights in the near future.

In 2003–04, Andrei Kirilenko became the first player in NBA history to post at least 5 points, rebounds, assists, steals, and blocked shots in the same game two times in one season.

TIME LINE

1967 Seattle joins the NBA as an expansion team, and Denver, then known as the Rockets, begins play in the American Basketball Association (ABA)

1970 The Portland Trail Blazers are founded

1974 The Utah Jazz are founded

1976 The Denver Nuggets join the NBA

1977 Portland wins the NBA title in the franchise's seventh year, defeating Philadelphia 4–2 in the finals

1979 The SuperSonics win their first Pacific Division title and the NBA title

1983 Utah wins a division title and qualifies for the playoffs for the first time

1989 The Minnesota Timberwolves join the NBA

2003 Minnesota wins a division title for the first time

2005 Seattle wins the division championship in the Northwest's first year

STAT STUFF

TEAM RECORDS

TEAM	ALL-TIME RECORD	NBA TITLES (MOST RECENT)	NUMBER OF TIMES IN PLAYOFFS	TOP COACH (WINS)
Denver	*1,486–1,604	0	*23	Doug Moe (432)
Minnesota	562–718	0	8	Flip Saunders (391)
Portland	1,535–1,303	1 (1976–77)	26	Jack Ramsey (453)
Seattle	1,659–1,425	1 (1978–79)	22	Lenny Wilkens (478)
Utah	1,347–1,163	0	20	Jerry Sloan (849)

*includes ABA

NBA NORTHWEST CAREER LEADERS (THROUGH 2004–05)

TEAM	CATEGORY	NAME (YEARS WITH TEAM)	TOTAL
Denver	Points	Alex English (1980–1990)	21,645
	Rebounds	Dan Issel (1975–1985)	6,630
Minnesota	Points	Kevin Garnett (1995–2005)	15,681
	Rebounds	Kevin Garnett (1995–2005)	8,601
Portland	Points	Clyde Drexler (1983–1995)	18,040
	Rebounds	Clyde Drexler (1983–1995)	5,339
Seattle	Points	Gary Payton (1990–2002)	18,207
	Rebounds	Jack Sikma (1977–1986)	7,729
Utah	Points	Karl Malone (1985–2003)	36,374
	Rebounds	Karl Malone (1985–2003)	14,601

MORE STAT STUFF

MEMBERS OF THE NAISMITH MEMORIAL NATIONAL BASKETBALL HALL OF FAME

DENVER PLAYER	POSITION	DATE INDUCTED
Larry Brown	Coach	2002
Alex English	Forward	1997
Dan Issel	Center	1993
John McLendon	Coach	1979
David Thompson	Guard	1996

PORTLAND PLAYER	POSITION	DATE INDUCTED
Clyde Drexler	Guard	2004
Drazen Petrovic	Guard	2002
Jack Ramsay	Coach	1992
Bill Walton	Center	1993
Lenny Wilkens	Guard/Coach	1989

SEATTLE PLAYER	POSITION	DATE INDUCTED
David Thompson	Forward	1996
Lenny Wilkens	Guard/Coach	1989

UTAH PLAYER	POSITION	DATE INDUCTED
Gail Goodrich	Guard	1996
Pete Maravich	Guard	1987

Note: Minnesota does not have any members of the Hall of Fame (yet!).

Alex English was the NBA's top scorer in the 1980s.

GLOSSARY

.500 mark—the same number of wins as losses; .500 is a winning percentage, which is calculated by dividing the number of victories by the total number of games

assists—passes that come immediately before a player makes a basket

bona fide—genuine or authentic

expansion team—a new franchise that starts from scratch

free agent—an athlete who has finished his contract with one team and is eligible to sign with another

inaugural—the first one

NBA Finals—a seven-game series between the winners of the NBA's Eastern and Western Conference championships

playoffs—a four-level postseason elimination tournament involving eight teams from each conference; levels include two rounds of divisional playoffs, a conference championship round, and the NBA Finals (all series are best-of-seven games)

prototype—an original on which later versions are patterned

swingman— a versatile athlete who can play more than one position (usually guard and forward)

Western Conference—one-half of the NBA, the Western Conference includes three divisions: the Northwest, Pacific, and Southwest. The Eastern Conference includes the other three divisions: Atlantic, Central, and Southeast.

FOR MORE INFORMATION ABOUT
THE NORTHWEST DIVISION AND THE NBA

BOOKS

Firsh, Aaron. *The History of the Denver Nuggets.* Mankato, Minn.: Creative Education, 2002.

Firsh, Aaron. *The History of the Portland Trail Blazers.* Mankato, Minn.: Creative Education, 2002.

Firsh, Aaron. *The History of the Seattle SuperSonics.* Mankato, Minn.: Creative Education, 2002.

Firsh, Aaron. *The History of the Utah Jazz.* Mankato, Minn.: Creative Education, 2002.

Hareas, John. *Basketball.* New York: DK Publishers, 2005.

Hudson, David L. *Basketball's Most Wanted II: The Top 10 Book of More Hotshot Hoopsters, Double Dribbles, and Roundball Oddities.* Washington, D.C.: Potomac Books, Inc., 2005.

Nichols, John. T*he History of the Minnesota Timberwolves.* Mankato, Minn.: Creative Education, 2002.

Owens, Tom. *Basketball Arenas.* Brookfield, Conn.: Millbrook Press, 2002.

Thornley, Stew. *Super Sports Star Kevin Garnett.* Berkeley Heights, N.J.: Enslow Publishers, 2001.

ON THE WEB

Visit our home page for lots of links about The Northwest Division teams:

http://www.childsworld.com/links

Note to Parents, Teachers, and Librarians: We routinely verify our Web links to make sure they are safe, active sites—so encourage your readers to check them out!

INDEX

ABOUT THE AUTHORS

Ted Brock has been writing books and articles about sports since 1972. He was a senior editor and staff writer with NFL Publishing and has taught sports writing at the University of Southern California. He has written for the *Los Angeles Times* and helped produce Web sites for the 2000 Summer Olympic Games and the 2002 Winter Olympic Games.

John Walters is a former staff writer at *Sports Illustrated* who worked at the magazine from 1989 to 2001. He is the author of two other books, *Basketball for Dummies,* which he cowrote with former Notre Dame basketball coach Digger Phelps, and *The Same River Twice: A Season with Geno Auriemma and the Connecticut Huskies,* which chronicles the women's basketball team's 2000–01 season.